For all at Auchterhouse Primary School—J.D.

First published in the United States by
Dial Books for Young Readers
A division of Penguin Putnam Inc.
345 Hudson Street
New York, New York 10014

Published in Great Britain by Macmillan Children's Books
Text copyright © 1999 by Julia Donaldson
Pictures copyright © 1999 by Axel Scheffler
Printed in China

3 5 7 9 10 8 6 4 2

Library of Congress Cataloging in Publication Data
is available upon request
Special Markets ISBN 978-0-8037-3371-8

The art was created using pencil, ink, watercolors,
colored pencils, and crayons.

This Imagination Library edition is published by Penguin Group (USA),
a Pearson company, exclusively for Dolly Parton's Imagination Library, a
not-for-profit program designed to inspire a love of reading and learning,
sponsored in part by The Dollywood Foundation. Penguin's trade
editions of this work are available wherever books are sold.

THE GRUFFALO

Julia Donaldson
pictures by Axel Scheffler

Dial Books for Young Readers New York

A mouse took a stroll through the deep dark wood.
A fox saw the mouse and the mouse looked good.
"Where are you going to, little brown mouse?
Come and have lunch in my underground house."
"It's terribly kind of you, Fox, but no—
I'm going to have lunch with a gruffalo."

"A gruffalo, Mouse? What's a gruffalo?"
"A gruffalo, Fox? I'm surprised you don't know!"

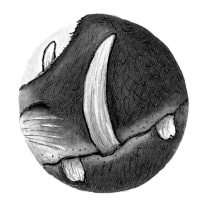

"He has terrible tusks,

and terrible claws,

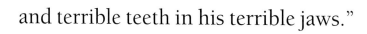

and terrible teeth in his terrible jaws."

"Where are you meeting him?"
"Here, by these rocks . . .
and his favorite food is roasted fox."

"Roasted what? Oh, my!" Fox said.
"Good-bye, little mouse," and away he sped.

"Silly old Fox! Doesn't he know?
There's no such thing as a gruffalo!"

On went the mouse through the deep dark wood.

An owl saw the mouse and the mouse looked good.

"Where are you going to, little brown mouse?

Join me for tea in my treetop house."

"It's frightfully nice of you, Owl, but no—

I'm going to have tea with a gruffalo."

"A gruffalo, Mouse? What's a gruffalo?"

"A gruffalo, Owl? I'm surprised you don't know!"

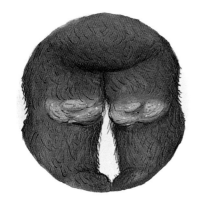

"He has knobbly knees,

and turned-out toes,

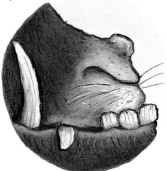

and a poisonous wart at the end of his nose."

"Where are you meeting him?"
"Here, by this stream . . .
    and his favorite food is owl ice cream."

"Owl ice cream? Too-whit! Too-whoo!
Good-bye, little mouse," and away Owl flew.

"Silly old Owl! Doesn't he know?
There's no such thing as a gruffalo!"

On went the mouse through the deep dark wood.

A snake saw the mouse and the mouse looked good.

"Where are you going to, little brown mouse?

Come for a feast in my log-pile house."

"It's wonderfully good of you, Snake, but no—

I'm having a feast with a gruffalo."

"A gruffalo, Mouse? What's a gruffalo?"

"A gruffalo, Snake? I'm surprised you don't know!"

"His eyes are orange.

His tongue is black.

Sharp purple prickles cover his back."

"*Where are you meeting him?*"
"Here, by this lake . . .
  and his favorite food is scrambled snake."

"Scrambled snake? It's time I hid!
Good-bye, little mouse," and away Snake slid.

"Silly old Snake! Doesn't he know?
There's no such thing as a gruffal . . .

"Oh!"

But what is this creature with terrible claws,

and terrible teeth in its terrible jaws?

Are those knobbly knees and turned-out toes?

Is that a poisonous wart at the end of its nose?

Are those eyes orange? Is that tongue black?

Do sharp purple prickles cover its back?

"Oh, yes! Oh, no!
A GRUFFALO!"

"My favorite food!" the gruffalo said.
"You'll taste good on a slice of bread!"

"Good?" said the mouse. "Don't call me good!
I'm the scariest creature in this deep dark wood.
Just walk behind me and soon you'll see,
Everyone for miles is afraid of me."

"Oh, sure!" said the gruffalo, bursting with laughter.
"You lead the way and I'll follow after."

They hadn't walked far when the gruffalo said,
"I hear a slither in the grass ahead."

"It's Snake," said Mouse. "Why, Snake, hello!"
Snake stared hard at the gruffalo.
"Oh, shivers!" hissed Snake, *"Good-bye, little mouse,"*
and slid right into his log-pile house.

"You see?" said Mouse. "I told you so."
"Hard to believe," said the gruffalo.

They walked some more till the gruffalo said,
"I hear hooting in the trees ahead."

"It's Owl," said Mouse. "Why, Owl, hello!"
Owl stared hard at the gruffalo.
"*Boo-whoo!*" screeched Owl, "*Good-bye, little mouse,*"
and flew right up to his treetop house.

"You see?" said Mouse. "I told you so."
"You may be right," said the gruffalo.

They walked some more till the gruffalo said,
"I hear paws on the path ahead."

"It's Fox," said Mouse. "Why, Fox, hello!"
Fox stared hard at the gruffalo.
"Oh, help!" barked Fox, *"Good-bye, little mouse,"*
and scampered into his underground house.

"Well, Gruffalo," said Mouse, "don't you agree?
Everyone in the wood is afraid of me!
But now my tummy is beginning to rumble,
and my favorite food is . . . gruffalo crumble!"

"*Gruffalo crumble!*" the gruffalo said,
and quick as the wind he turned and fled.

Then all was quiet in the deep dark wood.

The mouse found a nut and the nut was good.